BLOOD BROTHER

In the President's Service Series: Episode 3

Ace Collins

Elk Lake Publishing
***Blood Brother**, In the President's Service*, Episode Three

Requests for information should be addressed to:
Elk Lake Publishing, Atlanta, GA 30024
Create Space ISBN-13: 978-1-942513-17-9

Cover and graphics design: Stephanie Chontos and Anna O"Brien
Editing: Kathy Ide and Kathi Macias
Cover Model: Alison Johnson
Photography: Ace Collins

Published in association with Joyce Hart Agent Hartline Literary Agency.

To Alison

CHAPTER 1

Saturday, March 21, 1942

9:19 AM

Washington, DC

The music blaring from the car radio was so loud Alison didn't hear the gunshot. So when her sister suddenly paused just in front of the car and then slowly dropped out of view, she had no idea why. But the pained and perplexed expression etched on Helen's face just before she fell told her something was horribly wrong.

Bolting upright, Alison yanked up the door handle and scrambled out of the yellow Packard. Her black pumps barely touched the rubber-ribbed running board as she rushed around the passenger-side front fender. She found her sister, awkwardly sprawled on the sidewalk, her right hand still grasping the sedan's massive bumper. Blood stained her jacket and blouse, and it was forming a dark puddle on the sidewalk.

"Helen!" Alison fell to her knees and placed her palm against her sister's face. "What happened?"

There was no response.

After taking a deep breath to steady her nerves, Alison pressed her hand against her sister's side. The rushing blood's wet warmth caused a chill to race down her spine. "Oh, Helen."

Someone must have shot her. But who would want to kill her sister? After all, the FBI had Reggie Fister in custody.

Her gaze jumped from the wound to Helen's face and back. *Think, girl! Get a hold of yourself. You took a first-aid course in college. What do I need to be doing?*

The most important task right now was to stop the bleeding. Alison ripped off her coat, balled it up, and pushed it against Helen's side.

Now she had to get her sister to a hospital.

She glanced around. The immediate area was void of life. There weren't even any cars rolling down the street. No one was walking a dog or riding a bike. Where was everybody?

Dear Lord, if ever you needed to send an angel, it's now. I need some help here!

Her head bobbed from side to side, scanning the surroundings. Not a soul appeared—human or angelic.

As the seconds rushed by, Alison fought an internal battle. Was she better off staying and continuing to press into the wound, trying to slow the bleeding, or should she race down the street and find someone who would call for help? She didn't know. But each moment that passed put her sister closer to death.

"Oh, Lord, please," she begged. "You have to help me."

From the corner of her eye, she caught movement. About

half a block down the street, a mailman emerged from behind a yellow-bricked apartment building less than a hundred steps away. The short, white-haired gentleman was sorting letters as if there were nothing else in the world that needed his attention.

When Alison cried out, he looked up. His face contorted in confusion, he froze in place, a half-dozen letters in each hand.

"Someone just shot my sister," Alison screamed. "Please get help."

As if hit by a bolt of lightning, the postman dropped the mail into his bag and hustled toward Alison. After taking a moment to assess the scene, he rushed across the street to a red-brick home. He raced up the house's six steps and rapped on the green wooden door until a portly, middle-aged woman pulled it open.

Alison couldn't hear the exchange between the two, but when the homeowner stepped out of the way to allow the postman in, she figured he must be calling for the police and an ambulance.

Turning her attention back to Helen, Alison pushed her hand more firmly against the coat, covering the angry wound. But were her efforts doing any good? Helen's eyes were closed, her mouth slightly open, her lips twitching. Blood was still pooling up on the sidewalk and now dripping off the curb.

Leaning close to her sister's face, Alison whispered, "Help's on the way. Just keep breathing." Yet her words rang hollow. Would help really get there in time? And was there anything they could do when they arrived?

This couldn't be happening. The danger was supposed to be over. The FBI had caught the only man who wanted to harm Helen.

Alison looked back at the house the postman had disappeared into. How long had it been? A minute? Five? She didn't know.

This was supposed to be a dream day. A few moments ago she was on her way to meet the president of the United States. Now she was watching the life drain from her only living family member.

With a start, she realized Helen was no longer moving. Even her lips were still. Gripped by panic, Alison touched her sister's neck. She couldn't feel a pulse. She moved her finger forward, then to the side. Still nothing.

Wait! Though the sensation was so weak she could barely feel it, it was definitely there. Helen's heart was still beating! At least for the moment.

As hopelessness transformed into a sliver of optimism, Alison heard running footsteps on the street behind her. A deep, out-of-breath voice said, "Help is on the way. How is she?"

Alison turned her eyes to meet those of the concerned postman. "I don't know. She's lost a lot of blood."

"What happened?"

"I'm guessing she was shot. But I didn't hear or see anything." Tears filled her eyes.

The sound of sirens brought Alison's attention to the street. A half-dozen blocks away, a police cruiser was closing in. A moment later, a red-and-white ambulance came into view behind it.

"Okay, Helen," Alison pleaded, her eyes still glued to the emergency vehicles, "stay with me. You're going to be all right."

As the two vehicles came to a halt, a pair of policemen and

three medical personnel leaped out. Alison's gaze fell once more to her sister. Helen's color was ashen, her lips blue, her hands limp.

CHAPTER 2

Saturday, March 21, 1942

9:19 AM

Washington, DC

Fister rose from his kneeling position at the open window, cradling the rifle in his arm. He'd done his job. Time to get out of here.

He glanced over his shoulder to survey the one-bedroom apartment he'd broken into. He needed to make sure he hadn't left any trace of his presence here.

The latest issue of *Life* magazine sat on a small table beside the entry. On the far wall was a photo of a woman and a little girl, both cute in a wholesome Midwestern sort of way.

He briefly allowed his mind to consider who they might be and what their families were like. They were alone in the photo. Was the man in their lives serving in the military? Maybe he'd died in the war. Many men had already paid the ultimate price, and a lot more would do the same in the next few years. Countless women would be left behind to raise their children alone. Was that the case here?

To his right was a small kitchen. Two glasses and two bowls in the sink hinted at a breakfast of cereal and either milk or juice. A pair of small black shoes indicated the little girl in the photo likely lived here with the woman.

Walking into the bedroom, he noted a small twin bed pushed against the wall and a double bed on the other side. He opened the closet door. All women's clothing. No man called this place home.

After closing the door, he ran a gloved hand over the dresser. Not a speck of dust.

For a moment, he longed to know more about the pretty woman who was such a good housekeeper. What was her story? What did her voice sound like? What color were her eyes?

In truth, the identities of the pair who lived here were unimportant. The fact that their home provided the best position from which to accomplish his job, and the fortuitous coincidence that they hadn't been home when he arrived, was all that mattered. It was time to move on.

He tossed the gun on the double bed, then strolled to the front door, unlocked it, and stepped out into the sunlight. After glancing both ways, he pushed his hands deep into his pants pockets and sauntered down the sidewalk to a 1939 Chevy coupe parked at the curb. He opened the green car's passenger door and eased inside.

"Let's go," he muttered to the raven-haired woman behind

the wheel.

Grace pushed the starter button, and the vehicle's six-cylinder stovepipe engine roared to life. Easing off the clutch, she slowly pulled the hulking auto into the street.

Fister flipped on the radio, and the strains of a new release by Alvino Rey and His Orchestra filled the car. He turned up the volume and hummed along with the tune.

After the hit song had finished, he said, "Do you suppose it's true?"

"What's true?" Grace asked as she eased the car from second into third.

"What that song says about Texas? I mean, do you think the stars at night are really that much bigger and brighter than the ones found anywhere else?"

"I wouldn't know," she mumbled as she stuck her arm out the window to signal a left turn. "I've never been to Texas."

"Neither have I." He laughed. "But I have reason to believe I'll get there soon."

The two rode in silence for several minutes. After the coupe had crossed the state line into Maryland, Grace brushed her shoulder-length hair away from her face and ran her tongue over her ruby-red lips. "Did you have to kill her?"

He shrugged. "It was necessary."

"Why?"

He studied the driver, taking in her ivory skin, deep-brown eyes, high cheekbones, and slightly square chin. This woman was beyond perfection. She demanded attention without asking for it. When she walked into a room, everyone else faded into the background. There were likely men who made a hobby of just watching her breathe.

But like a cobra, she was also deadly. Grace had a hot body but a cold heart, made even more ruthless by her genius-level IQ. She was the kind of woman you wanted to lure into the dark. But few who stepped into the shadows with this creature ever lived to talk about it.

He forced his eyes back to the road, as much to regain his concentration as to check on their progress. "The phone tap revealed that Helen was getting way too close to the truth. If she told the FBI what she found out this morning, the mission would have to be scrapped, and years of work would go down the drain. It's that simple."

"And you have no regrets?"

He shrugged and looked out at the meadow on his right. "Emotions have no place in our lives right now. There's business to be done, and that means difficult decisions need to be made."

"That sounds pretty heartless. I mean, you knew her pretty well, didn't you?"

"Yes, I did. And she was even more dangerous than you are."

Grace opened her mouth to reply, but her words were cut off by the sound of a siren. She glanced into her rearview mirror. "What should I do?"

"Pull over. Running would alert the cop that his life might

be in danger."

She eased off the accelerator and steered the car toward the shoulder. "You think they're onto you?"

Fister slipped his hand into his coat pocket and felt the Lugar he considered his best friend. "You were driving too fast. This is likely nothing more than a traffic stop." But if someone had seen too much, he wanted to be ready.

Fister glanced over his shoulder at the 1940 Ford patrol car. After parking behind them, the uniformed trooper got out and strode toward their car. He hadn't pulled his gun, and his expression seemed more disgruntled than cautious, so there seemed to be no reason for concern.

Grace rolled down her window, and the state trooper nodded at her, as if to assure her there was nothing to worry about. "You on your way to a fire?" he asked as he leaned over and looked into the car.

"Just got to talking and wasn't watching what I was doing," Grace replied in a calm tone.

The officer studied her face for a moment, then smiled. "Hey, you're Grace Lupino. I've caught your show at The Grove. Took my wife there on our anniversary. Boy, the only thing more beautiful than you is your voice. It's like listening to an angel."

"Thank you," Grace replied with a smile that showed a perfect set of teeth. "I hope you'll come back. I sing there every week, Thursday through Saturday."

He sighed. "'Fraid I can't afford to go a place like more than once a year."

Grace opened her purse and pulled out a small brass case.

After unsnapping the latch, she removed a business card and handed it to the officer. "Give this to the doorman. The show and dinner will be on me."

The officer whistled as he took the gift. "Wow. Thanks, Miss Lupino."

"And make sure you come back to the dressing room after my show. I'd love to meet your wife."

"I sure will." The trooper's grin nearly split his face. "Meg will go crazy when I tell her who I met today." He tucked the card into his shirt pocket. "But please remember to drive a bit more slowly. The speeds limits are lower now due to the war."

"I'll do that," she assured him.

As the policeman practically skipped back to his car, Grace turned toward her passenger and smiled. "You owe me one."

"You saved his life," he shot back, easing his hand from his pocket. "So the way I figure it, he's the one who owes you. Now, let's get moving. I have a plane to catch."

CHAPTER 3

Saturday, March 21, 1942

10:30 AM

Washington, DC

"What do we have?" Spencer Ryan asked as he hurried into Washington General's emergency room. The tall blond doctor locked his deep green eyes on the barely breathing woman lying on the gurney, probably in her late twenties or early thirties.

"Single gunshot wound to the midsection," replied the gray-haired nurse in her mid-fifties. "Entered four inches below her left shoulder and exited between the vertebral ribs. She's lost a lot of blood and is hemorrhaging internally. Vitals are weak but steady."

"Get a blood type and then move her to surgery."

"We already have a blood type," Sally said. "She's B-negative. We only have a couple of units on hand."

Ryan shook his head. "We're going to need more than that."

As the hospital team pushed the patient out of the room

toward the surgery wing, Sally said, "I'll do my best to find some. This is one patient you really need to save."

He gazed at her. "What do you mean?"

"Her name is Helen Meeker. She works for the president. The White House has called twice in the past five minutes, asking for updates on her condition. This woman might well be the most important patient you've treated in your career."

Ryan rubbed the cleft in his square chin with his forefinger. If the president was keeping close tabs on this person, that likely meant the shooting had political implications. "Sally, call the White House and have them send Dr. Cleveland Mills over here to assist me."

"He's already on his way." She winked at him. "Apparently FDR thought Mills was the right man for the job too."

"Then find me some more B-negative blood," Ryan barked as he pushed through the curtains and down the hall.

"Yes, sir."

As he marched toward the surgery wing, Ryan sensed he was about to face the most crucial moment in the thirty-five years he'd been alive. Regardless of the outcome, his life would likely never be the same after this. If he was successful, FDR would forever be on his side. If he failed ... he didn't even want to consider that option.

CHAPTER 4

Saturday, March 21, 1942

11:22 PM

Washington, DC

Clay Barnes strolled up the sidewalk toward the FBI forensic scientist examining the scene where Helen Meeker had fallen. Dressed in gray slacks, a black blouse, and flats, the petite blonde in her early thirties stooped beside a dark pool of blood, studying the 1936 Packard parked at the curb.

"You need a coat," Barnes suggested as he noticed her trembling in the chilly air.

"Left it in the car." Her Southern accent gave away her Arkansas roots. "Why did the Secret Service send you over? This is an FBI crime scene. Even the local police have been pushed out."

Barnes shrugged. "FDR wants to make sure Hoover does a good job on this one. As a matter of fact, he's the one who told the director to assign you to the case. I'm glad old J. Edgar followed through."

Rebecca Bobbs stood. "I was wondering why they let me out of the lab." Her gaze focused on a window about a hundred yards to the east.

"Is that where the shooter was positioned?"

"Yeah. He broke into the lower-level apartment of a young widow named Jane Sims. She was working at a local department store, and her daughter was with friends. It was an easy lock to pick." She pointed toward the building. "Third window from the left. That's the apartment's living room. Evidence shows he only shot once."

"Any prints?"

"No," she replied, her gaze still locked on the window. "It was a professional job all the way … except for one thing."

Before Rebecca could explain, two FBI field ops wandered near, taking measurements and jotting down notes. She remained silent until the pair had moved up the street.

"Helen's sister was in the car, but she didn't see anything. Didn't hear anything, either, which isn't surprising. No doubt the gun had a silencer."

"Any other witnesses?" Barnes asked.

"No." Rebecca shook her head. "How's Helen?"

"Out of surgery, but it doesn't look good. She lost a lot of blood, and there was considerable internal damage."

Rebecca frowned. "I figured that, based on the large pool of blood by the car."

"And she's a rare blood type. B-negative."

Rebecca's deep blue eyes shot to Barnes. "B-negative?"

"Yes."

"I need to get back to the lab." She turned suddenly and jogged toward her car.

Barnes chased after her. As she pulled the driver's door open, he caught her by the arm. "You said there was something that made you question this being a professional job. What was it?"

"I'll tell you later." She climbed behind the wheel. "There's something important I have to do now."

Barnes held his position between Rebecca and the open car door. "The president needs to know what you know."

She slipped the key into the ignition and hit the starter. The motor roared to life. "The rifle was left at the scene. Just casually tossed onto the bed."

"So?"

"It was a Karabiner 98." Rebecca reached for the door.

Barnes remained in her way. "Isn't that what German soldiers carry in the field?"

"You know your foreign weapons."

"But how did it get here?"

"I don't know. But Hoover thinks it means the Nazis put a hit out on Helen and one of their men pulled the trigger."

"Seems logical."

"That's the problem. It's too open-and-shut. No, something else is going on here."

"Why do you think that?"

"Writing it off as an enemy hit means the FBI will shut down the investigation. They'll figure he's dropped into the shadows and has been spirited out of the country. So they won't bother looking for him. I'm guessing whoever did this knows that."

Barnes nodded, impressed with Rebecca's keen mind. "I'll make sure the president sees through the blind."

"You better." She reached around him and grabbed the interior door handle. "Now can I get back to the lab?"

He took a half-step back. "What's the big rush?"

She glared at him. "Helen Meeker is my oldest and dearest friend. We've both been so busy lately we haven't seen each other as much as we'd like. But she needs me more now than ever." She swallowed a lump in her throat. "I just hope I can deliver in time."

CHAPTER 5

Saturday, March 21, 1942

3:30 PM

Chicago, Illinois

Stepping out of the 1938 Plymouth, Fredrick Bauer wrinkled his nose as the unique aroma that defined the stockyards filled his senses. Turning up the collar on his dark overcoat, the tall, thin man strolled over to a fence and looked out at the livestock. With his hands pushed deeply into his pockets, he considered the events of the day.

A U-boat had sunk a tanker within twenty-five miles of the North Carolina coast. That attack had shaken millions to the core. As Nazi subs attacked again and again off the American East Coast, nervous throngs wondered how long it would be until Hitler landed troops here.

The fools didn't realize that Germany cared nothing about America. They wanted to control Europe. The U-boats were simply taking the nation's focus off the main prize.

Bauer heard a car roll into the gravel lot behind him. Rather than turn around to see who had joined him in this lonely part of the Windy City, he continued to look out over the sea of cattle.

Footsteps crunched in the gravel behind him. "They came a long way to die," the visitor noted wryly.

"Not as far as Americans have traveled to fight in a war and probably die." Bauer turned to face his guest. "I see you're still wearing black suits."

"As are you," the man replied.

Bauer shrugged. "Somber colors fit our job. After all, we decide who lives and who dies." He turned back toward the cattle pens. "How long have we known each other, James?"

The short, stocky man ran his hand through his closely cropped red hair and shrugged. "Maybe five or six years."

"It's actually been seven," Bauer corrected him. "You'd been with the FBI for just five months when I gave you your first tip."

"Melvin Purvis was impressed with the information."

Bauer yanked his hands from his pockets, leaned his elbows against the fence, and intertwined his fingers. "And Purvis made sure Hoover knew he could depend on James Killpatrick. A few dozen tips later, you pretty much started calling your own shots. I hear folks call you Bloodhound Jim for your ability to sniff out clues."

The small man smiled. "If you want me to admit I owe you big time, I do. I just don't understand how you get all this information about gangs and Nazi agents."

Bauer eyed James. "There's a lot of things you don't know

about me, Jim." Bauer gave a wry smile. "Not that you haven't tried."

"What do you mean?"

"You've dug everywhere you can, trying to figure out who I am. You've even tried a half-dozen times to have me followed." Bauer pointed his finger into Killpatrick's face. "If you ever tail me again, I'll be sending flowers to your funeral. Do you understand?"

James nodded meekly.

"Good. Now, I asked you here to give you the goods on a doctor in Chicago who's a Nazi agent. In fact, he was behind the mess with Fister trying to kill FDR and Churchill."

"You know about that?"

"I knew before you did. Now, do you want the information or not?"

"Of course." James looked at his right foot, which was pawing at the dirt.

"All right, then. This doctor has been working with the Nazis for years. He funnels information and money to agents, and he's the conduit to getting the information they gather back to Germany. Walk back to my car with me and I'll give you the file containing all the information you need to arrest and convict him."

Bauer ambled to the Graham sedan, reached in through the open driver's window, pulled out a folder, and handed it to the agent.

James's eyes widened as he reviewed the first page of material. "Dr. Eric Snider is one of the most respected men in

Chicago social circles."

"True. But he has no real practice. And yet there are millions of dollars in his bank account. Makes you wonder, doesn't it?"

"But—"

"The information in that file links Snider to everything, including the shooting of that woman in Washington this morning."

James's gaze shot up to Bauer's face. "You mean Helen Meeker?"

He smiled. "I knew about that before you did too. According to this material, Snider ordered the hit as a personal favor to Hitler."

"My Lord," James whispered.

"Snider is out of town right now, but he'll be back tomorrow night. Make your raid then. I would suggest after dark. I'm sure you'll uncover evidence linking Snider to a host of open espionage cases."

James narrowed his eyes at Bauer. "What do you get out of this?"

He grinned. "A chance to live an adventurer's life and help my country in the process."

"Won't you let me tell Hoover about your contributions this time?"

Bauer chuckled. "I've never wanted the spotlight. I'll leave that to you. I just want the satisfaction of seeing my work carried out." Bauer opened the car door and slid in. "Good-bye, James."

He smiled as he pulled out of the parking lot. One possible broken link in his chain was about to be eliminated. A second meeting this evening should prove just as fruitful.

CHAPTER 6

Saturday, March 21, 1942

6:30 PM

Washington, DC

Carrying a sealed metal box, Rebecca Bobbs strode into the hospital. Pushing through the waiting room and past the front desk, she continued down the hall until she reached the critical-care nurses' station. Behind the desk sat a white-clad woman, perhaps forty, with dark hair and a stern expression.

"You aren't allowed to be in here," the nurse barked.

Rebecca ignored the gruff warning. "I need to see the physician in charge of the Helen Meeker case."

"Why?" The large woman rose from her chair and crossed her arms over her ample bosom.

"I'm a forensic expert, and I'm working with the FBI. I believe I have something that will aid in Miss Meeker's recovery."

"You aren't a doctor."

"No, I'm not." She placed the metal case on the counter. "Now, I'm going to ask you again, who's in charge of this case?"

"Spencer Ryan," came the blunt reply.

"I need to talk to him."

"He's on rounds."

"Get him over here. Now."

The nurse stood straighter. "You have no right to make demands of me."

Rebecca exhaled a frustrated sigh. "Helen Meeker, who happens to be my friend, is in grave condition. Every minute we waste could cost her life. I have something here that might at least buy her some time."

The nurse gazed at her as if considering the strong words.

"You know, in my line of work I've learned about all kinds of foolproof ways to murder someone and never get caught."

"Is that a threat?"

"Nope, just a fact. Now, are you going to call the doctor or not?"

The nurse glanced at the metal container, then finally picked up the phone. "Dr. Ryan, you're needed at the critical-care nurses' station."

Rebecca crossed her arms over her black coat and tapped her foot. The bulldog in the nurse's uniform sat down and began leafing through files.

A few moments later, heavy footsteps sounded down the hall. A man in white jogged their way. "What is it, Nurse Kelly?"

The woman stood and pointed at Rebecca. "This person claims to be from the FBI. She's demanding to speak to you."

The doctor turned his attention to Rebecca. "What's so important?"

She picked up the metal container and nodded down the hall. Once they were out of earshot of the nurses' station, she stood close enough to Dr. Ryan to whisper. "I worked the crime scene where Helen Meeker was shot. I know she lost a great deal of blood. I also know her blood type is B-negative. I doubt you have enough on hand."

Dr. Ryan frowned. "You know a great deal about something that supposedly had a lid on it."

She nodded. "I have a supply of B-negative blood from the FBI lab."

"That's very kind of you, but we have a sufficient amount for Miss Meeker. Now, if you'll let me get back to my job—"

Rebecca grabbed his arm to stop him. "This blood was taken from a Nazi agent who infiltrated the British military. It's … for lack of a better word … supercharged."

"I beg your pardon."

"The man was shot, and his wounds healed so quickly we couldn't fathom it. We don't know if it's a natural phenomenon or if he was part of some kind of German experiment. But I have a pint with me. I think it might give you the edge you need to save Helen."

Dr. Ryan rubbed his hand over his mouth, glanced down the hall toward a closed door, then slowly moved his gaze back to Rebecca. "How can I be sure you aren't some crackpot?"

She whipped out her badge and showed it to him. "I know this case inside out. I've already shared information that hasn't been released to the newspapers. And you can call the FBI and check out my story. But that would take up precious time. Besides … they don't know that I borrowed this blood from them."

His eyebrows shot up. "You stole it?"

She shrugged. "They can get more. They have the man in custody. If I knew where he was, I would've brought him down to serve as a live donor."

The doctor pinched his lips together. "I don't know about this."

"What have you got to lose?"

"My license." He glared at her. "Look, even if I tested the blood and found it to be a suitable match for Miss Meeker, I'm not the only doctor involved in this case. Another guy is calling the shots now, on orders from the president. He never leaves the patient's side. He's even posted a guard inside the room."

The guard didn't come as a surprise. But who was this second doctor? "How well do you know this man?"

"I just met him today. But I've known about him my entire career. He's a legend. I've always wanted to work with him. He's the president's personal physician."

Rebecca smiled. "Dr. Cleveland Mills."

"You know him?"

"Quite well, actually. He operated on me before he went to work for FDR. And I've asked him a host of questions over the years about cases I've worked on. He likes me. More important, he'll believe me."

Ryan nodded. "All right. I'll take you to him. But this whole thing still sounds squirrelly to me."

"I'm sure it does," Rebecca said as she accompanied the doctor down the hall. "But in times of war, new discoveries are made more quickly than during periods of peace. In the next few years we'll no doubt see medicine advance almost as quickly as we see advances in man's inventions to kill."

CHAPTER 8

Saturday, March 21, 1942

10:30 PM

Gary, Indiana

Fredrick Bauer opened the small wooden chest and examined its contents. He ran his hand over a million dollars in faceted white diamonds before shutting the lid and looking back to his host.

"Will that do?" the man asked.

Bauer smiled at the tall, athletically built man in his forties. Ralph Mauch was not someone to mess with. A generation before, he had been a heavyweight boxing champ in Europe. Even now it appeared the blond man with the piercing blue eyes would have no problem going at least five rounds against the likes of Joe Lewis.

"Where did they come from?" Bauer asked.

"If you're asking if they can be traced, the answer is no. These gems were looted when the Nazis marched into Paris.

They have no connection to anything in this country. You can do whatever you want with them."

Bauer nodded, shut the lid, and put the box back on the table in Mauch's small study. "Have one of your men take the chest to my car. I'll trust your assessment on how much they're worth."

Mauch leaned back in the oversized leather-backed chair and crossed his muscular arms over his dark-green sports coat. His expression was a strange mix of admiration and disgust. "You would have earned a great deal more if you'd delivered on the big job."

Bauer shrugged. "Who would've thought the woman would figure things out? She wasn't even supposed to be there. We had her on a wild goose chase. She simply got lucky."

"I don't believe in luck," Mauch replied, his voice harsh and cold. "You plan, you prepare, and you execute. That's how it works. Your problem was Fister. Still is. He simply can't be controlled. He's too unpredictable."

"I didn't pick him," Bauer shot back. "Your people delivered him to me."

"We don't like that business in Washington this morning either," Mauch warned. "Shooting Meeker serves no purpose."

"You didn't order that?" Bauer asked.

"No."

"I didn't either."

Spotting a copy of *Gone with the Wind* on Mauch's bookshelf, Bauer stood and retrieved it. Running his fingers over the spine, he turned to Mauch. "Have you read this?"

"No, but my wife has."

"I'm partway through it now." Bauer returned to his chair, still holding the book. "I hear it's an all-time best seller. I think that says a great deal about this country, don't you?"

Mauch smoothed his hair with his right hand. "Fredrick, if you didn't order the hit on Meeker, who did?"

Bauer frowned. "I have no idea. But I have a contact who might."

Mauch rubbed his brow. "Let me know what you find out." He glanced at a newspaper sitting on a table to his right. It was filled with the latest images and stories of battles on both fronts. "Who do you think is going to win this war?"

"We are," Bauer asserted. He let his response linger for a moment before pulling an envelope from his coat pocket. "This microfilm contains plans for a new American plane. It's experimental, so who knows if it will ever go into production? But there might be elements of it that Berlin could take, refine, and put to use."

"Doesn't sound like a game-changer to me," Mauch argued. But he plucked the envelope from Bauer's hand anyway. "Hitler has two other things he wants more. And you have promised to deliver them."

"I'm close on both counts. It's just a matter of finding the right moment to get them." He sighed. "But as far as I can tell, they're worthless. The words on those papers are nothing but myths."

"Try telling that to Hitler," Mauch scoffed. "He's bought into all that mystical stuff. I mean, he actually believes De Soto stumbled onto something of great power during his 1541 exploration of America."

"If it was that powerful, why did the guy who found it die on the trip? Shouldn't his discovery have kept him safe?"

"What you and I believe isn't important. The only thing that matters is what that crazy man in Germany believes."

Bauer stared at the microfilm in Mauch's hands. "At least that will buy us some time until I can get what the old fool really wants. But playing with the occult is not going to cancel out his stupid decision to invade Russia."

"Time will tell."

"Well, time is money, so have your people put that chest in my car. I need to get back home."

"And where is home for you, my friend?"

"That's something you'll never know. And take my word for it, it's far better that you don't."

CHAPTER 9

Sunday, March 22, 1942

8:33 PM

Chicago, Illinois

James Killpatrick and three other men, all dressed in dark suits, tan overcoats, and hats, stepped out of the black 1940 Lincoln Zephyr and walked to the gates of the palatial white-stone mansion owned by one of Chicago's most respected citizens. A long driveway winding through a half-acre of manicured lawn led up to the home's main entry. Except for two lit windows on the far right side of the ground floor, the two-story structure appeared lifeless.

"You sure this is the place?" asked a tall man in his late twenties.

Killpatrick looked back over his shoulder into the man's eyes. "You read the file. This is Snider's home."

"Yes, sir," came the apologetic reply.

He gathered his team close and outlined their mission in hushed tones. "We've been here for an hour, and no one has entered the home except Snider. He's not expecting us, so he likely won't be armed. I'd rather we do this without fireworks, but have your guns ready just in case."

His men nodded.

"Now, listen up. Hoover wants this guy alive so we can find out what he knows. These men are like a cancer—you have to find it all if you want to be healthy." Killpatrick paused, studying his team. "Any questions?"

"How do we get through the gate?"

Killpatrick smiled. "Follow me." He led the trio to the iron entry and pointed at the latch. "Notice anything?"

"It's not locked," said the agent who'd asked the question.

"Good observation, Price."

The young man lifted the latch, and the gate swung open. "How do you know all this stuff? No one at the Bureau gets dirt on folks like you do."

"It's a gift. Now, let's go."

Killpatrick crept up the lane toward the entry, his team following close behind. When they reached the porch, he climbed the two steps and raised his finger to the doorbell buzzer. But he didn't press it.

"Something wrong?" Price asked.

"The door is slightly ajar." He turned to his men. "Keep out of sight, but have your weapons ready. Better to blow a hole in your coat pocket than to have someone blow one in you." He grinned wryly. "Ruins your coat either way."

He punched the buzzer. No response. He repeated his action

with the same results.

Pulling his revolver, he eased the door open with his foot and stepped inside a large, dark foyer. "This is the FBI. Come out with your hands up."

Hearing nothing, he reached to the right of the door and felt along the wall for a light switch. Finding one, he flipped it on.

To his right was a living room; to his left, a dining room. Both extravagantly furnished. And apparently empty. But a light shone through an open door on the far side of the living room.

"You think he's in there?" Price whispered.

"He could be anywhere. But my old Sunday school teacher always told me to follow the light. So that's where we're going first."

As he moved toward the living room, he whispered, "Green, you move to the right. Price, you take the left. Johnson, watch our tail. We don't want anyone coming up behind us."

Killpatrick moved slowly past a large couch, a huge stone fireplace, and a Zenith console radio, keeping his eyes on the partially open door. Taking a position just to the right of the entry, he peered inside.

The room was small, no more than fifteen by fifteen, and likely used as a study or library. A lit brass lamp sat on an oak desk in the middle of the room. Two padded red leather chairs flanked the floor-to-ceiling bookshelves to the left. The door hid everything to his right.

Killpatrick signaled Green and Johnson to cover both sides of the entry. Keeping his gun at waist level, he pushed the door with his left hand. As it slowly opened, he noted a small yellow love seat. A man lay sprawled awkwardly against one of the arms, blood dripping from a wound in his forehead. His limp right hand held a gun.

"One victim," Killpatrick announced in a hushed tone. "Move in together on my signal." He waited a second, then nodded.

As Killpatrick approached the man on the love seat, Price walked to the desk and looked behind the large oak rolltop. "Got another one. And he's alive."

After knocking the gun away from the first victim's hand, Killpatrick moved to Price's side. The man on the floor had been badly beaten. His face was cut, swollen, and bruised; both eyes were black. While his breathing was steady, he appeared to be unconscious. A pistol rested on the floor about a foot from his right hand.

After slipping his weapon back into his shoulder holster, Killpatrick dropped to one knee and turned the man's face toward him.

"Either of these guys the one we're looking for?" Price asked.

"They both are."

"What?"

"The one on the couch is Dr. Snider. This man is Henry Reese."

"The missing agent?" Green asked.

"That's right." Killpatrick checked Reese's pulse. "Henry, can you hear me?"

The beaten man's eyes fluttered and opened. "Bloodhound?"

Killpatrick chuckled. "Yeah, it's me, buddy."

"Where am I?"

"In Chicago. More specifically, you're in the home of Dr. Eric Snider. My guess is you killed him."

A concerned look filled Reese's battered mug. "I did?"

"Don't worry about it. He was a spy. He deserved it. Now, rest easy. We need to get you to a doctor. A real one." He turned to his men. "Green, call an ambulance. Price and Johnson, you two go through the house and see if anyone's hiding somewhere. If you find anybody, shoot first and ask questions later."

After his men rushed off, Killpatrick glanced at the dead doctor. So much for delivering Snider to Hoover for questioning. But at least Henry Reese was alive.

CHAPTER 10

Monday, March 23, 1942

9:30 AM

Washington, DC

Rebecca Bobbs strolled by the nurses' desk and smiled at the stern-looking woman behind the counter. The woman shot back a hateful glare.

"Nice to see you again, too, Nurse Kelly," she said, then made her way down the hall to room 172. She knocked lightly. The door opened and a uniformed man appeared in the entry.

"Rebecca Bobbs. The doctors are expecting me."

The muscular, six-foot-tall policeman stepped to one side, allowing her to enter. The room was just like a thousand other critical-care units. Helen Meeker, pale but breathing steadily, lay in the bed in the center of the room, eyes closed and lips slightly open.

"She's much better," said one of the two doctors standing on the far side of the bed. "I wouldn't have believed it was possible, but there was something in that blood transfusion that accomplished a lot more than we could do through our best medical procedures."

"That's what I figured." She turned from Dr. Ryan to the older man. "Give it to me straight, Doc."

Cleveland Mills shrugged. "She's not out of the woods yet. But a day ago I didn't give her one chance in a hundred. Any way you can get us some more of that blood?"

She nodded. "I convinced the FBI to draw more from the prisoner we got the first batch from."

"Great." Mills smiled.

"There's just one problem."

"What's that?" Ryan asked.

"This batch is normal B-negative. There's nothing special about it."

"How is that possible?" Mills asked.

"I don't know. Neither does anyone else at the lab. But the wound on the man's hand isn't healing at a faster rate than anyone else's would. Maybe he was exposed to something just before we drew blood the first time. Or perhaps he was taking some kind of drug before we picked him up, and he's no longer taking it. All I know is that incredible healing factor isn't there anymore."

Dr. Ryan placed his hand on Rebecca's chin and lifted her face until their eyes met. "You saved her life with what you gave us. She experienced a week's worth of healing in a single day."

She forced a smile. "I hope you're right. But now the only supply of blood that might have saved countless other lives is gone." She looked at the other doctor. "In saving my friend, did I doom a million others?"

Cleveland Mills touched her shoulder. "You did what you felt was right at the moment. Given the choice, I would have done the same thing. And so would the president."

Rebecca closed her eyes for a few moments, trying to relish the realization that her friend might live after all. Her justification did little to remove her overriding sense of guilt.

She turned back to the men. "I'm a scientist. Even though my expertise is in solving how people died or committed crimes, I've always considered myself a part of making the world better for the living. Somehow we stumbled on something that had more potential for healing than anything on this planet. Given time and thorough study, we might have found a way to re-create it. But rather than think of future generations or the men on the battlefield, I selfishly thought of my friend and how much I'd miss her if she died." She gazed at Helen. "I don't think she'd respect that kind of thinking."

The doctor walked up to the guard. "Would you mind stepping outside a second?" He turned to Dr. Ryan. "You as well. I need a moment alone with Miss Bobbs."

"Of course." The younger doctor shuffled toward the exit. After the two men left, Mills closed the door and then signaled for Rebecca to join him by the window.

"Becca, you and I know this blood came from Reggie Fister. But the president doesn't want anyone else to be aware of that fact."

"I wasn't going to give away his identity. Most people at the

FBI don't even know he's still alive."

The doctor nodded. "I spoke with the president today. Apparently something's happened to Fister. He seems confused and lost. He's like an addict whose mind has been deeply affected by a long period of drug use. The doctor in charge described it as going through withdrawal. Perhaps he's coming down from the drug that supercharged his blood."

"Is that what you think?"

"I don't know what to think. But if the Nazis managed to arrange for Fister's medical miracle, they might be able to do it on a huge scale. The Germans could put together an almost invincible army."

Rebecca stared at her shoes. "I really messed up, didn't I?"

"I don't see it that way. And neither does the president. Fister's blood fix was temporary. And now he's a physical wreck. So there are obviously problems with the process."

Rebecca turned to stare at Helen. "Will she go through withdrawal too?"

"There's no way to tell at this point. But while we're waiting to see what happens, we need to figure out who tried to kill her."

He made a valid point.

"Since this seems to be a matter of national security, the president has come up with a plan. I've convinced him to include you in it. He wants you to return to the White House with me."

"I'll need to inform my superiors at the lab."

"They've already been told."

"What about Helen?"

"Dr. Ryan will take good care of her. And he'll let me know

if there's any change in her condition." Mills caught her eye. "This mission is dangerous, Becca. You could end up like Helen … or worse. It's your decision whether to accept it or turn it down."

Rebecca smiled grimly. "I'm more than ready to do my part. I want to pick up where Helen left off."

"That won't be necessary." Mills steered her toward the door. "We already have someone to do that job."

CHAPTER 11

Monday, March 23, 1942
10:18 AM
Chicago, Illinois

Henry Reese's head was beginning to clear, but his memory remained as foggy as a fall night in London. He simply couldn't explain where he'd been or what he'd done in the last several days. Even after a good night's sleep and two meals, he was still drawing blanks. He felt as if he'd been sleepwalking for a week.

This was more frustrating than anything he'd ever known. He was failing, not just as a person but as a professional.

His fellow agents had been sitting in his hotel room with him for hours, but he was unable to provide them with any leads. They'd have been better off talking to a three-year-old.

"Ballistics tests prove you fired a gun," Killpatrick said for the tenth time. "And a bullet from the gun you had in your hand killed Snider. You must remember firing it."

Reese raised his palms. "How many times do I have to tell you? I don't even know who Snider is. I have no idea how I got into that house, and I sure don't remember shooting him."

He ran his hands through his hair, doing his best to unearth whatever memories he could. "I can remember things that happened two weeks ago as clear as day. And I remember everything from this morning." He moaned. "I could tell you the names of every kid in my grade-school class and even give you most of their birthdays. I can give you details on my investigation of the January sixteenth plane crash in Nevada. I know how many folks were on the flight, where it took off, the names of the crew. But for the life of me, I don't remember anything about Snider."

"What's the last thing you recall before waking up here?" Killpatrick asked.

Reese dredged his disheveled memory banks. "Being in a gunfight while chasing a guy named Andrews. Someone slugged me. I don't know anything after that."

Killpatrick paced the small hotel room, clearly trying to get some mental traction.

"Can't you fill me in on what happened to me?" Reese finally asked.

The agent sat in a desk chair and loosened his gold tie. "That guy you were chasing, Andrews, ended up in the same room with FDR and Churchill."

"Did he try to kill them?"

"No. He tried to save them. It was Reggie Fister that tried to kill them."

"Fister?" Reese stared at the other agent in disbelief.

"Would have done it too, but Helen shot him first."

"Is he dead?"

"No. But we have him in custody and he won't talk."

Reese pushed out of bed and walked to the mirror. The dark circles under his eyes almost met his lips. His skin was pale, his eyes bloodshot, and a week's worth of beard growth covered his face. He'd seen corpses that showed more life.

Reese turned away from the glass. "What else can you tell me?"

Killpatrick took a deep breath. "Somebody shot Helen."

Reese's breath caught in his throat. "Is she alive?"

"Last I heard, she was hanging on. But she's unconscious. And since Fister's in custody, no one knows who tried to gun her down."

"Who else would have a reason to kill her?"

"We don't know. But we suspect Dr. Snider ordered the hit. Now that he's dead, we can't interrogate him. We were hoping you could give us a lead."

Reese groaned. "I wish I could."

"Maybe something will come to you."

"I hope you're right."

"Why don't you get cleaned up? We'll catch the next flight back to DC. Hoover wants an update on what you were working on just before you were abducted." He paused. "Do you remember what that was?"

"Yeah, I do," Reese answered. "And he's not going to like what I found out."

CHAPTER 12

Monday, March 23, 1942

11:19 AM

Washington, DC

Clay Barnes eased down on the corner of his desk and studied the three guests seated in front of him. They hardly seemed qualified to capture a killer. But Alison Meeker, Rebecca Bobbs, and Dr. Cleveland Mills were the players the president wanted on the team.

Who would've thought he'd be depending on a trio of civilians to apprehend the person who'd tried to kill one his closest friends? But the FBI was too busy to put their full weight behind it, and the local police had nothing to go on. He was not about to let this case grow cold, like so many other murders in this country. And neither was the president.

His guests were bright, willing, and even eager, but they were not trained. One of the women was a college kid, the other a person who knew her way around a lab. Neither of them weighed more than 115 pounds. The old doctor was a good man in surgery, and he'd fought in World War I. But how good would he be in a knife fight?

These people had lives. Friends. Hobbies. Family. Unlike him, they likely turned their radios on for something other than news once in a while. And unlike him, they probably had something to live for. Was it fair to put them in harm's way?

None of that mattered. FDR had approved the plan, and there was no turning back now.

He tossed a newspaper into Rebecca's lap and waited for her to read the headline: "Helen Meeker, FDR Aid, Shot. Out of Surgery and Expected to Be Released Tonight."

The woman looked up. "I was just in her room. She wasn't even conscious. She's in no condition to be released."

"No, she isn't. But we need whoever shot her to believe she is. According to that article, you and Dr. Mills will be accompanying Helen to her apartment, where you'll both monitor her recovery."

Rebecca handed the paper back to him. "I don't understand."

Barnes dropped the copy of *The Washington Post* on the desk and made his way to a window overlooking the White House's north lawn. He jammed his hands into his pockets and studied the gray sky. "Here's the plan. The three of you will go to the hospital at separate times during the day. Alison, you'll put on your sister's clothes. Tonight, you'll all leave together. A police escort will lead you to the apartment. Shortly thereafter, the protection will seemingly disappear. If the assassin comes out of hiding to finish the job he started, we'll capture him and gain the information we need in order to find out why Helen was shot and who ordered it."

"Why am I involved?" Rebecca asked.

"You're one of Helen's closest friends. People would expect you to be with her during a time like this. Also, you know how to handle a gun."

"True." Rebecca crossed her legs and smoothed her skirt. "But I'm no match for a hired killer."

"He won't know that." Barnes winked.

"Look, I'm fine with being there," she said, "but Alison's a kid. Why risk her life?"

"Actually, this was my idea," the young woman said. "If whoever shot my sister thinks I got a good look at him, my life is in danger as long as that wacko is out there."

"Exactly my point." Rebecca raised an eyebrow at Barnes. "Couldn't we bring in some pros from the Secret Service for this charade? Alison should be taken as far away from here as possible. You could even put a guard on her."

Alison clenched her trembling fingers. "I think I'd be safer in the apartment with you and the doctor than anywhere else."

"So does the president," Barnes added. "But there's another issue at work here. Helen has long believed there's a mole at the White House. If we use our regular staff for this job, the mole may find out this is a setup."

Rebecca sighed. "So you've leaving it up to the three of us to catch this menace?"

"Actually, there'll be another man in the apartment with you.

He's flying back to Washington right now. We'll make sure he's in place before you leave the hospital. He's volunteered for the job, he has a vested interest in seeing it through, and he knows Helen well."

Rebecca narrowed her eyes at him. "And who's that?"

Barnes straightened. "Henry Reese."

A collective gasp filled the room. "He's alive?" Rebecca shrieked.

"He's a little rough for wear. But he wants to nab the guy who shot Helen, and the president wants to give him that chance. The doc said he's in good enough shape to pull this off. And since we haven't announced that Henry's been found, no one at the White House will know he's there."

As the trio digested the surprising bit of news, Barnes moved back to the window. There was something else at play here too, something that directly involved Rebecca Bobbs. But he'd wait to reveal that until after this assignment was finished.

CHAPTER 13

Monday, March 23, 1942

5:15 PM

A farm outside Springfield, Illinois

"Why'd you do it?" Fredrick Bauer demanded.

Fister, outfitted in a blue suit, white shirt, and gray tie, smiled. "Two reasons. First, she was onto the truth. The phone taps you instigated proved it."

"You should have let me take care of that." Bauer got up from the divan of his rural home and stood directly in front of his cocky guest, who'd parked his keister in an overstuffed green chair.

"I was the better man for the job. After all, how can the FBI suspect someone they already have in custody?"

"And what was your second reason?"

"She embarrassed me." Fister scowled. "No woman does that to me."

Bauer glared at the disgusting excuse for a human being.

"Well, she might just do it again."

"What are you talking about? Helen Meeker's dead."

"She's getting out of the hospital tonight."

"That's impossible. I hit her with a kill shot."

"But your blood, engineered in my labs, enabled her to recover."

Fister shook his head. "I need to get over there and finish her off."

"Oh, no, you don't. You're staying right here."

"But—"

"I've got a man in DC who can do the job. And he's not some self-absorbed spy who lets his emotions override his good judgment. He has a long and perfect track record with organized crime."

"And what if your Mr. Wonderful doesn't get the job done?"

"Then I have a backup plan, of course. I *always* have a backup plan." Bauer shook his head. "You know, for a man Germany invested years of training in, you can be a real idiot. You couldn't have done this job on your own. Who helped you?"

Fister sneered. "A friend."

"Give me a name."

"Grace Lupino."

"Oh, that's just great." Bauer threw his hands up in disgust. "I spent years getting her into the perfect spot to gather information and go unnoticed, and you go and do something that might expose her."

Fister grinned. "I didn't expose her. She's still a Washington club singer."

"If she's compromised," Bauer barked, "I will never be able to replace her." More than once that woman had managed to get information no one else could. And he had a very important assignment for her down the road. "I don't want you to ever contact her again. You got that?"

"Sure," Fister chirped. "Now, when are you going to take out Helen Meeker?"

"Tonight." After inhaling a deep breath to calm his emotions, Bauer returned to his chair. "I do have a job for you, one that's more up your alley."

"What's that?"

He grabbed an eight-by-ten photo off the end table and tossed it into Fister's lap. "That man is Jacob Kranz. He's one of the world's top economists. He escaped from Germany in 1935. He's living in New York now, and Hitler wants him back."

"Why?" Fister asked, studying the picture.

"Kranz is using his wealth to help fund the resistance in Germany. He even underwrote a failed assassination plot on Hitler. The Nazis want to put him on trial and then publicly execute him for treason."

Fister sneered. "There's no way to kidnap a man like that and smuggle him back to German. Not when there's a war going on."

"Hitler doesn't want excuses. He just wants the job done." Bauer tapped his fingers on the desk. "Besides, this will buy us some time on the bigger things the Nazis are expecting me to accomplish."

Fister leaned back in his chair and crossed his right foot over his left knee. "So, how do we do the impossible?"

"Kranz has a daughter who goes to school at the University of Texas. She's enrolled under a false name: Suzy Miller. Kranz has been careful never to be seen with her in public, so few people know about their connection. You nab the girl and take her to our base in south Texas. Once she's safely there, we'll contact Kranz and give him a choice. Either his daughter is smuggled back to Germany, where she'll be placed in a concentration camp, or he changes places with her."

Bauer handed Fister a photo of the coed.

He grinned. "She's kind of cute."

"Her mother was an actress, and the girl inherited her looks."

Fister's eyebrows rose. "Can I take some … liberties with this job?"

"There won't be any chaperones, so feel free to enjoy yourself. Just make sure she's alive to talk to her father when the time comes."

"When do I leave?"

"We'll get you on a train tomorrow. You'll be staying in the Texas Inn, just off campus. One of our mute friends will meet you there with a car. Take your time scoping things out. When you have the girl, your connection will provide you with a plane and a pilot to fly you to a ranch close to Brownsville." He crouched in front of Fister, his nose inches from the man's face. "And Reggie …"

"Yes?"

"Don't shoot anyone. Is that understood?"

"I promise, this will be clean."

"It better be. If it's not, you're going to end up in a concentration camp or in front of a firing squad."

CHAPTER 14

Monday, March 23, 1942

9:30 PM

Washington, DC

Alison, wearing a large floppy hat and an oversized trench coat, was wheeled from the hospital to Helen Meeker's yellow Packard. After taking her place in the backseat, she was joined by Dr. Cleveland Mills. Rebecca Bobbs slid behind the wheel, then followed the 1941 Ford police sedan to her sister's apartment.

Once everyone else was inside, two uniformed policemen helped Alison to the door. After speaking briefly with the doctor, the pair got back into their squad car and roared off into the night.

"How's Helen?" a deep voice asked.

Alison switched on the lights, revealing a man in a dark suit, light blue shirt, and black tie.

"Henry," Rebecca said with a smile, her blue eyes lighting

up. "It's good to see you alive. I should have known nothing can harm you."

He opened his arms to the blonde. After a long hug, he stepped away, nodded to Alison, and reached out his hand to the doctor. "I'm Henry Reese."

"Cleveland Mills. But you can call me Doc."

"What can you tell me about Helen?"

"When I looked in on her this morning, she seemed slightly improved. She's been moved to a remote room that only three people are aware of, including the young doctor who's taking care of her. She should be perfectly safe there."

"I hope so."

"What do we do now?" Rebecca asked.

"We wait." Reese shrugged. "At some point, one of the bad guys will likely try to enter this apartment with the intention of overtaking Dr. Cleveland and kidnapping the woman they believe to be Helen Meeker." He nodded at Alison. "What they won't know, hopefully, is that I'm here too." He pulled a gun out of his shoulder holster. "And I'll be ready for them."

Alison gulped. Part of her hoped these guys would make their move soon so this could all be over with more quickly. She didn't know how long she could sit and wait, imagining everything that could go wrong.

CHAPTER 15

Monday, March 23, 1942

10:30 PM

Washington, DC

Louise Kelly crept down the dimly lit hallway, glancing left and right to make sure she wasn't being observed. When the white-clad nurse reached the right room, she paused in the doorway. Seeing no one in either of the chairs or beside the bed, she entered, silently closing the door behind her.

She was hours later than planned, but this was the first time the room hadn't had someone in or near it. Dr. Ryan had been pulled away less than an hour ago to perform emergency surgery on a car-wreck victim, finally giving her the chance she'd been waiting for.

Well, as her mother always said, better late than never.

Louise reached into her pocket and pulled out a syringe as she moved quietly to the bed. She hadn't been fooled by the deception. She'd known Helen Meeker was in no shape to go home. And now the woman never would. That knowledge caused her both a twinge of guilt and a great sense of relief.

In the dark room, she reached out her gloved hand and felt for the patient's arm. Finding it, she pushed the tip of the needle into the shoulder area and engaged the plunger.

After dropping the instrument back into her pocket, Louise headed back toward the door. No one would ever suspect her. The cause of death would be listed as complications due to a severe gunshot wound. It was the perfect crime. By the time Spencer Ryan came back to check on Meeker, she'd have been dead for at least two hours.

As she reached for the door handle, a low voice whispered, "Why did you do that?"

Whirling to her right, Louise tried to penetrate the darkness in a far corner, but she saw only shadows. "Who's there?"

"You have a long tenure of service at this facility, without a single blemish on your record."

Louise shuddered. Who was the person behind those haunting whispers? She couldn't even tell if it was a man or a woman. But clearly whoever it was knew something about her.

"Why would you try to murder a patient?" the soft voice asked.

Louise wanted to run, but fear held her in place, squeezing her heart and stealing her breath.

"You must have been paid a lot of money."

"That's not true," she blurted out. "Someone else's life depended on it."

"Whose?"

Beads of sweat dotted Louise's upper lip. "I—I can't tell you."

"You'd better. If you don't, you'll be on your way to jail within minutes."

Louise sank into the nearest chair, fighting both fear and tears. "They have my daughter. They told me they'd kill her if I didn't do as they asked. Hannah's only sixteen. She's all I have. If she dies, I might as well die too."

"Are you supposed to call them when you've finished the job?"

"No. They told me they'd know by midnight whether Helen Meeker was dead, and if so, they'd let my little girl go. They must have someone watching."

The hidden voice sighed. "Go back to your station and stay there until someone discovers the body."

"My shift is over."

"Then go home and wait for your daughter."

Feeling as if she'd been freed from a cage, Louise stood quickly and opened the door. She barreled out of the room and down the hall without looking back.

As she scurried through the lobby, a beautiful raven-haired woman nodded to her before disappearing into a stairwell leading to the basement.

CHAPTER 16

Tuesday, March 24, 1942

1:30 AM

Washington, DC

Henry Reese was listening to the radio playing Glen Miller's *A String of Pearls* and flipping through an issue of *Life* magazine when a knock on the front door brought him to high alert. After grabbing his gun from where it rested on the coffee table, he signaled for Rebecca Bobbs to answer. As she moved toward the entry, the agent backed into the dark bedroom.

"Who is it?" Rebecca asked.

"Clay Barnes," came the muffled reply.

Rebecca glanced back to Dr. Mills on the far side of the room, then at Alison seated in a chair at the kitchen table, and finally turned toward Reese, standing mostly out of sight behind the bedroom doorway. He nodded.

After flipping the latch, she eased the door open. A second

later three men pushed hard against the entry, knocking the woman to the ground.

"Nobody move," the tallest one barked, aiming a Luger at the doctor.

"Who are you?" Rebecca demanded as she pushed off the floor into a kneeling position. "And what gives you the right to barge into my friend's apartment?"

The man grinned, his pallid complexion revealing he'd spent little time in the sun. "That's none of your business," he announced, his voice gruff and coarse.

The intruders closed the door behind them, then scattered throughout the room, each of them picking out a target. Noting the silencers on the guns and the gang's composed nature, Reese realized this was not a fly-by-night raid. These men were seasoned and prepared, and the leader was an experienced hit man Reese recognized. Even if he surprised them, he wouldn't be able to take out all three before they at least winged a victim or two of their own. And if he shot too quickly, he might hit one of his own people.

Time to play a bit of poker.

Reese emerged from the shadows, his gun aimed at the leader. "When did Rusty Cline start working for the Germans?"

The trio's gaze collectively flew to the agent.

"If any of you moves, Cline gets it between the eyes."

"Don't drop your guns," Cline ordered. "We've got him outnumbered." He peered closely at Reese, keeping his gun sighted on Alison. "Do I know you?"

"My name is Henry Reese, and I'm with the FBI."

Cline shrugged.

"I thought you were muscle for the New York mob. You freelancing for the Nazis now?"

"I don't know anything about Nazis. But I do know you could only get one of us before we shot you, the woman, or the old man."

"I've got backup," Reese bragged.

Cline cackled. "We've been watching this place for hours. You're the only one here." He smiled. "I, on the other hand, have a fourth member on my team, and he has a gun aimed at you through the bedroom window."

Was Cline bluffing? Reese couldn't afford to look behind him to find out. If there really was a guy out there in the darkness, the outcome of this lethal game was already decided. And since he'd told the FBI and Secret Service not to get too close so as not to scare anyone off, he was to blame.

The only question was who would shoot first—and how many would die before the gunfire ended.

"Drop your weapon, G-Man," Cline ordered.

"I don't think so," Reese growled. "I can at least get you, and likely one more."

"But you'll die too."

"I die either way. You're not going to let anyone walk out of here alive." That was Cline's MO. And why he'd never served time or been killed. "I have you in my sights. If the guy behind me makes a sound, I'll blow your brains out. So your side may win the war, but you'll lose the battle. Have you considered where you want to be buried?"

Cline swallowed hard, but didn't take his gun off Alison.

Reese inched a bit closer. "Even if you somehow survive, you won't get paid. Helen Meeker's not here."

Sweat appeared on the man's brow as he took a closer look at Alison.

"That's her sister."

"What are you trying to pull?"

Reese pointed to the newspaper on the table. "Helen's picture is right there on the front page."

"Keep him covered," Cline shouted to the unseen man behind Reese. He compared the photo in the paper to the young woman he had targeted. Then he fixed his gaze on Reese. "What's going on here?"

"You're the one who fell into a trap, Cline."

The hood shook his head. "I knew this job was too clean."

"Look, there's no reason anyone has to die here. If you tell me who sent you, I'll let all of you walk away. If you're ever caught by the cops, you'll have a chip you can play because you helped the FBI today."

"It's not that simple," Cline muttered. "I was told to leave no witnesses. If I do, I won't live long enough to get caught for anything." He cocked his gun.

From the corner of his eye, Reese saw Rebecca push off the floor and reach for the light switch. A second later, the room went black.

In the sudden darkness, Rebecca bolted at Cline. Her shoulder slammed into him, and he tumbled forward as she grabbed for his weapon.

With catlike reflexes, he jabbed an elbow into her chin and rolled to his right. He was rising to one knee when a flashlight beam caught his chest. A shot rang out, and Cline crumpled to the floor.

The beam found one of Cline's men, and another shot rang out, catching the man in the wrist and knocking the gun out of his fingers. He collapsed with a scream, writhing and clutching his hand.

The flashlight went dark.

"Let me hear your weapon hit the floor," demanded a gravelly voice a few feet to Reese's right.

A moment later, the sound of something heavy hitting the carpet echoed through the room.

"Put your hands on your head," the voice ordered.

"They're there."

The flashlight came back on, proving the man's claim.

"Becca," Reese said, "give us some light."

When the room was once again illuminated, Cline lay in a fetal position on the floor, his blood staining the green carpet. One of his men stood in the corner, his hands on his blond mop of hair. The other intruder was trying to stop the profuse bleeding coming from his right wrist.

Beside the door, Rebecca held a gun she'd retrieved from one of the men. Dr. Mills still sat in his seat, observing Cline's wound. Alison leaned against the kitchen sink.

On Reese's right, holding a flashlight in one hand and a gun in the other, stood Helen Meeker, her dark eyes shining and a grin framing her pale face.

CHAPTER 17

Tuesday, March 24, 1942

1:50 AM

Washington, DC

Helen Meeker surveyed the room. After confirming that the bad guys were all incapacitated, she caught her sister's adoring gaze. "Alison, you okay?"

"Yeah."

Meeker turned to Rebecca. "It's great to see you again, my friend. It's been far too long."

"I thought you were in a coma," Reese said with an ear-to-ear smile.

"And I thought you were dead," Meeker quipped. "You look terrible. If you've taken up boxing, you should quit now, while you still have a somewhat straight nose."

While Reese gathered up the rest of the thugs' firearms, Meeker watched Dr. Mills ministering to Cline's wounds.

"How's he doing?"

"He won't live very long."

After handing her Colt to Rebecca, Meeker stooped beside the dying gunman.

"You're good," he murmured.

"Are you the one who put the bullet in my gut last Saturday?" she asked, hoping he'd want to clear his conscience before his time ran out.

Cline shot her a painful grin. "If I'd done it, you wouldn't be here."

"Then who did?"

"I don't know. I was just sent in to clean things up."

"Who sent you?"

He shook his head.

Reese knelt beside Meeker. "You working for the Nazis?"

"I'm not that low." Cline's eyelids fluttered and closed. A few second later he stopped breathing.

Meeker stood and turned to Rebecca. "Call the Bureau. Let's get these others in custody."

Reese rose beside her. "I take it you found the guy outside the bedroom?"

She shrugged. "I put him to sleep, then opened the window and climbed in to save your bacon."

"I saw her," Rebecca said. "She signaled me, then stepped back into the shadows. I'm just glad I figured out she wanted me to turn the lights out."

Dr. Mills walked up to Meeker. "When you came out of your coma this afternoon, I told you not to leave your room."

"And if I'd followed your orders, the president would be looking for a new doctor."

"All this blood for nothing," Reese grumbled, gazing around the room.

"Maybe not."

"What do you mean?" Mills asked.

"There was another attempt on my life today."

Alison gasped.

"I managed to foil it with the help of a good-looking doctor named Spencer Ryan. He put a rather lifelike mannequin in my bed. When the nurse who was forced to try to kill me came in, she was wearing rubber gloves, so she couldn't tell it wasn't a real arm she injected poison into. Spencer is with her now. Once her daughter is returned home safely, he should be able to get the rest of the story out of her. Maybe even the telephone number for her contact."

"Spencer, eh?" Reese asked, a hint of jealousy in his tone.

"Yes." Meeker winked. "Did I mention that he's really good-looking?"

"You did," the agent grumbled.

Meeker clapped her hands. "All right, folks. Let's get this mess cleaned up."

CHAPTER 18

Tuesday, March 24, 1942

7:30 AM

Springfield, Illinois

Fredrick Bauer parked his car outside the train station and studied the passengers walking into the depot. Most were young men in uniform, strolling toward an adventure that would soon take them into harm's way.

Bauer glanced at Reggie Fister, sitting in his passenger seat. "Those boys have no idea what's in front of them. Most of them aren't coming back. This might be the last time they see their folks or their hometown. They may never have another date or even drive a car."

"Who cares?" Fister sneered. "They're just war machinery. They can be replaced."

Bauer raised an eyebrow. "Like you?"

Fister's lip curled. "Oh, I'm special, don't you know."

Bauer ignored Fister's bragging, still focused on the

servicemen waiting on the platform. "Look at those expectant faces. They think they're off to do God's work."

Fister frowned. "You know better than that."

"Of course. But the war promoters have to sell it as something noble. I mean, the Nazis have rewritten the entire Christian faith to make Germans the chosen race, the only ones who truly represent God. That's how they justify their actions. Since it was Jews who killed Christ, that makes every Jew the enemy. So murdering them by the millions is touted as divine."

Bauer watched a young man in an Army uniform kiss his crying sweetheart good-bye. "Do you think Hitler really believes that Jesus was the Son of God, thereby making his crucifixion such a heinous crime?"

"I doubt it." Fister shrugged. "But as long as the men fighting his wars believe it, that's all that matters."

Bauer pulled his gaze away from the group of deluded soldiers. "America and Britain aren't much better. They're saying that Germany represents Satan, and that their countries are the world's moral voice. They wrap up the Bible in a red, white, and blue flag and send their children off to die, as if this war is a holy crusade. They quote Scripture and preach sermons on patriotism, claiming that killing millions of Germans is furthering God's plan for this world."

Fister eyed him with curiosity. "And what about the Japanese?"

"They believe God is behind them as well, and that the rest of the world is heathen and therefore doesn't deserve to live."

"And do you consider yourself any better?"

"At least I don't evoke God's name to justify my actions. I know what I do is selfish and evil. But I don't kill randomly. I do it with purpose."

"So that makes you the noble one?"

"No." Bauer chuckled. "It just makes me practical."

"Who do you think will win the war?"

Bauer considered the question carefully. "The Germans and the Japanese have the will to win, but the Americans have the resources. And the wisest leaders."

"You think they're smarter than Hitler?" Fister asked in a low voice.

"Instead of staying focused on a war he could win, he invaded a country that offered him nothing but stubborn resistance." Bauer pulled a cigarette out of his pocket. "Still, Hitler might have survived his ill-advised attack on Russia if Japan hadn't drawn the United States into the war. Neither country can win against an enemy with the resources the US has."

Fister turned his gaze to the depot. "Then what are we doing here?"

"I think you're in this because you're an adventurer. When the Germans were training you, you bought into their beliefs, to a certain extent at least." Bauer narrowed his eyes at Fister. "There's no doubt in my mind that they removed your soul. You have no hint of a thread of morality, which makes you perfect for this work."

"And you?"

Bauer pushed in the car's cigarette lighter. "I have no allegiance to any flag, country, or leader. The war offers me opportunities to make money and gain power off the misfortunate of others. No matter who wins, I will not only survive, I'll thrive."

Fister rubbed his jaw. "Is it too late for me to join your team?"

Bauer laughed. "I doubt Hitler would let you work for me. Within a few days, you'll be taking either Kranz or his daughter back to Germany. You'll be a hero in Hitler's eyes. He'll probably keep you by his side until the bitter end. And then you'll likely die in a hail of bullets. Won't that be glorious?"

For the first time, Bauer detected a hint of regret in the tough man's eyes.

The lighter popped, and Bauer pulled it out and touched it to the end of his cigarette. Reggie Fister wasn't much different from those new recruits on the train platform. Just like them, he was headed off into the unknown. And Bauer didn't envy him one bit.

He took a long draw and exhaled a curl of white smoke. "It's time for you to go."

Fister brushed a speck of dust off the gray suit he'd been given to wear on his journey south. "I wish you could have come up with something better for me than this. Looks like it came from a second-hand store."

"It did. The last thing you need is to stand out in a crowd. And you'd better drop the British accent. You need to be just another American businessman."

"I know my cover." Fister straightened in his seat. "My name is Bill Johnson. I was born in Boston in 1915. Due to an injury suffered in a car wreck in 1938, I am not eligible for military service. I work at a law firm in Chicago." He shook his head. "Could I be more boring?"

"Just follow the script, and don't ad lib this time."

Fister grunted, then reached into the backseat, grabbed his suitcase, and stepped out of the car.

As Bauer watched his operative climb up onto the platform, he made a mental note. It was time to recruit a new adventurer.

CHAPTER 19

Tuesday, March 24, 1942

5:00 PM

Thurmont, Maryland

On FDR's orders, Helen Meeker and the rest of the people involved in the shootout at her apartment were flown to the presidential retreat at Camp David. After being checked out by Dr. Sterling Ryan, they were fed, shown to a bedroom, and told to get as much rest as possible.

When Meeker finally pulled her sore body out of bed, it was late afternoon. After dressing in dark slacks and a yellow sweater, she rummaged through the kitchen, made herself a turkey sandwich, and joined Henry Reese in the main living room. She sat in a leather chair, looking out over the expansive grounds.

"What happened to you after I was kidnapped?" she asked.

He shrugged. "I'm not sure. They tell me I was drugged. And that I might never remember what happened on those days."

Meeker pulled her aching feet up onto a stool. "I heard they found you in some doctor's house in Chicago."

"Yeah, with a gun in my hand. Apparently the one used to kill Snider. The files indicate he set up the hit on you and that he was Fister's boss. Guess that makes me a hero."

She studied his handsome but bruised face. "At least the swelling is coming down. You almost look human now."

He frowned. "I'm sure I'd remember shooting a guy. It had to be a frame."

"So who did kill Snider?"

He stood. "I don't know." Reese shoved his hands into his pockets and walked to the large window overlooking a small lake.

Helen joined him, pushed her arm through his, and leaned her head on his shoulder. "I'm just glad you're okay."

She was enjoying the warmth of his body against hers when she heard footsteps on the wooden floor. Releasing Reese, she turned and spotted a smiling Clay Barnes.

"Hope you two rested well," the Secret Service agent said.

"I hate that word," Reese grumbled. "Whenever anyone mentions *rested,* there's always a big job that needs to be done."

Barnes chuckled. "Helen, Dr. Ryan tells me you're fit for duty already. I hope if I ever get shot there's some of that blood around for me too."

"Better to just avoid being shot," she said. "I'm not proud of having Reggie Fister as my blood brother."

"Can't say I blame you there," Barnes quipped. "Now, if you two will follow me into the dining room, there are some things we need to discuss."

Reese and Meeker followed Barnes into the retreat's spacious dining room. Already seated around the large table were Alison, Rebecca Bobbs, Dr. Cleveland Mills, and Dr. Spencer Ryan. Meeker grabbed the open spot beside her sister. Reese took the chair between the two doctors.

Barnes walked to the head of the table and remained standing. "People, let me start by saying that each one of you possesses unique skills that make you valuable to your country. But those talents are yours. None of you has to volunteer to use them in the president's service."

Meeker shot a look at Alison. Her own job required that she do whatever was needed to help her country and the president. But her sister was a civilian, with no such demands on her.

Barnes glanced down at the files spread before him, tapping one with his index finger. "Except for Dr. Mills, none of you has any dependents. Your parents are dead, and except for Alison and Helen, none of you has siblings. I apologize for the harshness of this statement, but if any of you die, there won't be anyone to mourn the loss."

Meeker glanced across the table at Reese. When their eyes locked, he shrugged, apparently just as clueless about all this as she was. "Get on with it, Clay," Reese said. "What's going on here?"

Barnes looked up. "We have a couple of delicate problems that we need to address off the books."

"What do you mean?" Bobbs asked.

Barnes sat, resting his elbows on the table and folding his

hands. "If we do this, Rebecca and Henry won't be working for the FBI, Helen will not be aligned with the Secret Service, and Dr. Ryan will no longer be a practicing physician."

Murmurs filled the room.

Barnes picked up a photo and slid it down the middle of the table. "Can any of you tell me what that is?"

Reese glanced at the image. "Fort Knox."

"Exactly. And there's supposed to be more than twenty thousand metric tons of gold bars in that facility."

Meeker peered at Barnes. "What do you mean by 'supposed to be'?"

"Recent tests have proven that some of the gold bars transferred to Fort Knox over the past two years are not solid gold but gold plated. We estimate there may be a couple of million tons missing."

"How is that possible?" Reese asked. "Those shipments have all kinds of security checks. And the trains are heavily guarded from beginning to end."

"We believe the exchanges were made before the bars arrived at the train station. But we can't find any proof. Whoever did it covered their tracks well."

"No pun intended, right?" Meeker rolled her eyes.

"Only a handful of people know about this," Barnes continued. "Obviously, the team involved in testing at Fort Knox knows. I'm the only one in the Secret Service the president has told. He also shared it with Dr. Mills a couple of weeks ago."

No wonder the good doctor didn't seem surprised at the news.

"Not even Hoover is aware of what's going on here. If this were to get out, it would shake the confidence of our entire country, not to mention all the Allied nations."

"Do you think the Germans are behind this?" Alison asked.

"No. This started before we got into the war."

"Organized crime?" Reese suggested.

"Possibly. Three weeks ago, two men disappeared from their duty posts at Fort Knox. We haven't been able to find them."

Meeker's head was spinning. She couldn't imagine how all this was affecting the others in the room, especially Alison.

Barnes opened a file and pushed two more photos toward the middle of the long table. "The picture on my left is of Captain Ellis McCary. He's thirty-five, divorced, and has a spotless service record. The other is Master Sergeant Buster Rankin. He's twenty-eight, has no children, and his wife was killed in a hunting accident three years ago."

"And you think these two guys could pull off something this big?" Ryan asked.

"No. But they might be connected with the people who did." He took a deep breath. "At the same time McCary and Rankin disappeared, something else disappeared that's worth even more than the missing gold."

Meeker wondered what could be more valuable than all that gold.

Barnes moved to the side of the room and leaned on a large china cabinet. "On December 27, 1941, in anticipation of a possible attack on Washington, the original Declaration of Independence and the Constitution of the United States were removed from the National Archives and shipped to Fort Knox for safekeeping, along with the Magna Carta and many of the crown jewels of Europe."

Reese whistled.

"A recent examination of those documents proved that the Declaration of Independence and the Magna Carta that we have in our vaults are not authentic. They're copies."

The gravity of the theft sent the room into a deep silence for several minutes.

"The press cannot get wind of this. Not even Congress can know about it. Since we likely have a mole in the White House, we can't talk about it openly there. That's why you were all brought in."

Meeker had known this trip to Camp David had to be about more than just giving her and her companions some much-needed rest.

"Your job is to figure out who's behind this and quietly return those documents to Fort Knox. If you can accomplish that, there are several other missions the president would like you to team up on."

"You're asking us to become an intelligence unit," Reese noted.

"A secret one."

"What would that entail for us?" Bobbs asked.

"Alison would be moved into Helen's position at the White House, allegedly serving as an aid to the president. In truth, she would be the conduit for information to get from the team to the president and back. Dr. Mills would remain at his position and serve in a similar capacity."

Meeker glanced from Alison to Mills and back to Barnes. "And the rest of the team?"

"I'm an electronics expert. Henry is skilled in crime solving, explosives, and weapons. Spencer is a trained code breaker. Rebecca is the best crime-scene investigator and laboratory technician in the country." Barnes winked at Meeker. "And we all know what you can do."

"Well, I'm on board," Meeker announced. The rest nodded.

"Great." Barnes released a deep breath. "Now, how do you feel about being dead?"

"What?" Bobbs asked.

"In order to unravel this mystery, we need to be able to do our work in complete secrecy. Besides Alison and Dr. Mills, we all have people looking for us. So we'd need to send an announcement of our deaths to all the papers. The most logical story would be a plane crash. Once the war is over and the need for this unit ends, we can miraculously come back to life."

Meeker glanced around the room and smiled. "Guess this isn't a bad group to join in the tomb."

"Why not?" Bobbs chimed in

"I'm in," Reese added.

Ryan nodded. "Two beautiful woman, plenty of action and intrigue, hopefully a good budget. I can live with that. Or should I say, die with that?"

"Before you all sign on, there's one more thing that needs be addressed. FDR had in mind a very specific way this group was to function, and if the members don't all agree to it, then the team will be dissolved before it even begins."

"And what's that important little detail?" Reese asked.

Barnes took a deep breath. "The president insisted that Helen be in charge. We will all have to work under her orders. She has the president's confidence far more than any of us." He looked at Meeker. "I know Helen well, so I'm fine with that. But can the rest of you deal with having a five-foot-four-inch dynamo calling the shots?"

Ryan announced he had no trouble with that rule.

Reese looked into Meeker's eyes. She couldn't read what he was thinking. The room was still for one of the longest minutes of Meeker's life. Finally, the FBI agent nodded. The team was set.

CHAPTER 20

Thursday, March 26, 1942

8:10 PM

Austin, Texas

Dressed in a white shirt, tan jacket, and blue slacks, Reggie Fister enjoyed a stroll across the campus of the University of Texas. To most of the ten thousand students enrolled here, the war raging in Europe and the Pacific was little more than words in a newspaper.

On this mild spring night under a beautiful full moon, Fister carried two textbooks under his arm. Beneath his jacket he'd hidden a Luger.

He stopped beneath a live oak tree beside the Memorial girls' dorm and casually watched coeds enter and exit the residence hall. Finally, a short, full-chested brunette walked out the front door and stepped onto the main sidewalk. Fister sauntered up beside the nineteen-year-old. "Aren't you Suzy Miller?"

She stopped, her dark eyes studying Fister's face. "Yes."

"I think you're in my history class."

"I don't recognize you."

He grinned, then grabbed her elbow and pulled her against his side. "What you feel pressed into your ribs is a gun. If you so much as raise your voice, I'll pull the trigger. You don't want to die, do you?"

She shook her head.

"Now, at the end of this sidewalk, there's a white car parked at the curb. That's where we're going. When we get there, you'll get in on the passenger side and scoot over behind the wheel. I'll follow you. When I close the door, you'll start the car and pull away from the curb. I'll tell you were to go. Do you understand?"

"Yes," she whispered.

"All right, then. Let's start walking. Not too fast or too slow. Just act like we're on a date."

The girl moved down the sidewalk on trembling legs. When they were about halfway to the objective, three sweater-clad girls met them. "Hey, Suzy," a blue-eyed blonde said. "Who's your fella?"

"Just a friend," came the hushed response.

"Didn't know you had any friends like this." A short redhead smoothed her orange coat. "Aren't you going to introduce him?"

"I'm visiting from back home," Fister said. "We're going to grab a soda and catch up on old times. Aren't we, Suzy?"

The girl nodded.

"Don't do anything I wouldn't do!" The blonde laughed.

As the three marched off, Fister leaned close to Suzy. "You

played that real smart. If you continue to use your head, you'll live through this. And it'll make a great story for your grandkids. Now, keep walking."

Fifty steps later Fister opened the door of the 1938 Oldsmobile and signaled for Suzy to enter. After she was behind the wheel, he slid in and closed the door.

As the Olds coupe pulled away from the curb, the three coeds who had teased Suzy earlier stood in front of the dorm and waved. One of them screamed out, "Have a good time!"

CHAPTER 21

Friday, March 27, 1942

7:30 AM

Camp David, Maryland

At the president's suggestion, the new secret team stayed at Camp David while news of their deaths in a private crash was circulated in the media. Since the accident had allegedly taken place in a remote section of the Blue Ridge Mountains and a massive explosion had burned the bodies behind recognition, the stories soberly announced that a memorial service would be conducted at a later date.

Since neither Bobbs nor Ryan would be readily recognized, they headed out to the rural areas outside of Washington to find a suitable location for the group to live and work in.

While Reese sorted through the evidence gathered by the various intelligence agencies and military on the two missing men from Fort Knox, Meeker and Barnes met in the retreat's main study, engaged in a heated discussion.

"You're supposed to be dead," Barnes argued, his normally subdued tone nearly shaking the windows. "You can't blow your cover on day one. I'm sure the president will allow you to have him transported here."

"Look, this guy has knowledge that we need. And it won't matter if he knows we're alive. He's in solitary, for heaven's sake."

He pointed a finger at her face. "We can't take chances. We have to be smart."

Meeker gave him a sly smile. "The president put me in charge for a reason. Women sense things that men miss. Most of you are too proud to even ask for directions!"

"But what you're asking isn't at all logical."

She shook her head. "Look, Barnes, you're a bachelor, so you haven't been around females enough to know this. But there's one rule every man needs to learn, and that's to never doubt a woman's intuition."

The ringing desk phone created a momentary ceasefire. "You going to get that?" Meeker asked.

"Go ahead. You seem to have all the answers."

She picked up. "Camp David."

"Helen, it's Uncle Franklin."

She stood a bit straighter. "What can I do for you, Mr. President?"

"A student from the University of Texas is missing. Her name is Suzy Miller. The kidnapper told the girl's father that if legal authorities were notified, she would be killed."

"Typical."

"Helen, I'd like your team to work this."

She blinked. "But, sir … I thought we were supposed to be finding the missing documents. Isn't that more important than a kidnapping?"

"Normally, it would be. But Suzy Miller's real name is Susan Kranz. Her father escaped Nazi Germany six years ago. He's one of my economic advisers."

Meeker recalled meeting Mr. Kranz.

"Helen, they're not asking for money. They want to exchange the man for his daughter."

So this was somehow tied to the war.

"I want you to shadow Kranz, but don't give yourself away unless it's absolutely necessary."

"We'll do our best to save the child," Meeker assured him.

"A plane will be ready for your crew in four hours. I want every member of the team on this. Barnes can fly, so you won't need a pilot. The meeting point is Brownsville, Texas."

"Yes, sir."

"One more thing, Helen. Three coeds saw the man who took the girl. The description they gave matches that of the man you asked to be sent to Camp David so you could interview him."

Meeker's pulse kicked up a notch.

"I tried to talk Jacob out of going to Texas, telling him there's nothing he can do for his daughter there, and he might actually get in the way. But he flew down today. The kidnappers told him to check in to the Raleigh Hotel and wait for them to contact him."

"I'll join him there as soon as possible."

"Keep me informed, Helen. You can call my private line. Or call Alison at your old apartment."

"I will, sir. Good-bye."

She set the receiver back onto the cradle, then explained the situation to Barnes. "We need to talk to Fister before we leave. Bring him to Camp David immediately."

CHAPTER 22

Friday, March 27, 1942

9:15 AM

Camp David, Maryland

Meeker glanced across the hallway at Barnes. "You want to be in on this? Henry's joining me."

"Sure." He shrugged. "If he's going to see that you're not dead, he might as well know I'm not either."

"All right, then. Let's go see what we've got." The two of them entered the dining room.

Fister looked much better than he had the last time he was face-to-face with Meeker. His eyes were clear and there was a bit of color in his cheeks. Though he was dressed in a nice pair of blue slacks and a white cotton shirt, he lacked the charm that she'd noted in the British Embassy. Fister was no longer capable of owning a room with the power of his charisma.

Taking the chair across from him, Meeker held her tongue until the two men sat down on each side of her.

"Can we get you anything?" she asked, no doubt surprising her partners with her gentle manner. "Would you like something to eat or drink?"

"No, thank you," Fister answered quietly.

"I'm Helen Meeker. Do you remember visiting me the night you were captured after the train wreck?"

"No," came the emotionless reply. "I don't recall much about that evening."

"So this is the first time you've seen me?"

He nodded.

Barnes slammed his fist on the table. "We both saw you at the farm in New York when you tried to kill the president."

"No, we didn't," Meeker said. "We saw his identical twin. And the man who did escape from that train wreck realized I'd figured it out. That's why I was shot."

"There are … two of them?" Reese asked.

"After the parents died, Reggie was raised in Scotland, his father's native country, and the other boy in Germany. The twin who tried to kill the president and the prime minister is Alistair Fister." Meeker turned back to their prisoner. "Did you know you had a twin?"

"No one ever told me that."

"Orphanages often withhold information about siblings." She gazed at him with deep sympathy. "Where were you before you were taken to the train wreck, Reggie?"

"I was held in a laboratory of some sort. I escaped once. All I remember was that the land around it was flat. Lots of corn fields."

"Probably somewhere in the Midwest," Reese noted.

"Before that, I was in someplace dry and hot." Reggie ran his hand through his hair. "I was there for a year or more. The seasons didn't change much. But if the wind was right, I could smell salt air. Kind of reminded me of being on the coast back home."

"And before that?"

"I was held in Germany."

Meeker glanced at a clock on the far side of the room. Rebecca and Spencer would be back any minute, and the plane was on its way. They needed to get out of here within the hour.

"Reggie, would you like to help us catch the folks who were behind kidnapping you and holding you prisoner all these years?"

"Absolutely," he replied, a bit of life appearing in his eyes.

She turned to Reese. "We need to talk." Meeker excused herself from Reggie and walked out into the hall, followed by the agent.

"It sounds to me like Fister was held in south Texas before he was moved to the Midwest."

"Could've been California."

"Texas makes more sense. It's closer to the Midwest. I think we should take him with us and see if something triggers his memory."

"I don't know. Sounds risky."

"Well, we can't leave him here. Besides, we need him more than he needs us."

Reese shrugged. "You're the boss."

"You got that right."

"But first I need to ask Fister one more question."

"Lead the way."

They went back into the room, and Reese leaned forward on the table. "Reggie, did you ever see who held you?"

"Not in enough to light to make out features. Even when they talked to me, they stayed in the shadows."

"Did you ever hear them talk about plans or operations?"

"I overheard things a few times. But I couldn't make much sense of what they were saying."

"Did they ever talk about a plane crash in Nevada?"

Reggie smiled. "Yes. I remember a lady talking about a movie star dying in the crash."

"Carole Lombard."

"That's it! The lady was mourning the loss, but the man in charge told her there was something much more valuable on that flight and that was why it went down."

"Did you hear anything else?" Reese asked.

"Not about the crash. But I did hear them talking about a French explorer in Arkansas. I don't remember any details about that."

Reese grinned. "Reggie, you're going to Texas with us. If you remember anything along the way, be sure to tell one of us, okay?"

"Sure."

Back in the hallway, Meeker peered at Reese. "What was that all about?"

"I'll explain later." He wrapped his arms around Meeker and kissed her cheek. "Let's go to Texas!"

CHAPTER 23

Friday, March 27, 1942

Noon

St. Louis, Missouri

Fredrick Bauer wiped crumbs off the ripped vinyl seat of a back booth in the Downtown Diner before sliding into it. The small, cramped, noisy eatery was immersed in a thick nicotine cloud. With its greasy food and dirty floors, this was the last place anyone who was health conscious would want to visit. Which was precisely why Bauer chose it for his meeting with Ralph Mauch.

A former boxer, Mauch was a health fanatic. He worked out daily and carefully monitored everything he ate. He didn't allow alcohol or cigarettes in his home. He went to bed early and got up with the sun.

Bauer sipped coffee and listened to the tunes playing on the Wurlitzer jukebox for ten minutes before Mauch strolled into the establishment, with a frown so pronounced it made his whole face sag. Bauer stood and waved at his guest.

"I hate travel," Mauch muttered as he sat across the marred tabletop from Bauer.

"I enjoy it," he replied with a smile. "Being alone in a car gives me a chance to reflect on life as I take in the sights of this beautiful world we live in."

Before Mauch could respond, the plump waitress appeared at the table. The stains on her dress indicated she'd spilled nearly as much food as she'd delivered. "You boys want to hear about the special today?"

"No," Mauch grumbled. "Just bring me coffee … black."

"And you, sir?" Her voice revealed a bit of Midwestern charm tempered by a heavy dose of fatigue.

"Ham on rye."

"Chips with that?"

"That'd be fine."

After the woman waddled off, Mauch leaned across the table. "Why'd you pick this place?"

"We won't be noticed in a crowd. None of the patrons here will be able to describe us after we leave. Besides, I like watching Americans rushing around. They're always in a hurry. Even when they eat. Look at that guy, for example." He pointed to a table across the aisle, where a man sat alone, wolfing down a sandwich while reading the newspaper and humming along with the jukebox. "As soon as he's finished with his meal, he'll hastily pay his bill and practically sprint back to his office."

"So?"

"You're the same way. Always in a hurry to get things done.

And what good does all that rushing around do? You should relax and enjoy life."

"We're in a war, remember?" the former boxer growled.

"No, we're not. A lot of other folks are. But nobody's shooting at us. We're thousands of miles away from falling bombs and the smell of constant death."

The waitress brought Mauch's coffee and Bauer's order. When she was out of earshot, Mauch whispered, "What have you got to report?"

"We have the girl." Bauer bit into his sandwich. "This is good. You should get one. My treat."

"Where is she?"

"Texas." Bauer savored another bite. "This is the best ham I've had in years. As good as anything you'll find in the Black Forest."

"What about Kranz?"

"He's flying down today. You can tell Hitler he'll have a house guest soon."

"What's going to happen to the girl?"

Bauer shrugged. "How she dies will be decided after we get Kranz on the U-boat."

Mauch appeared to relax. "And the papers?"

"They were on the plane when it went down. My sources tell me no files were recovered, so they're probably still there." Bauer sighed. "Too bad Lombard had the misfortune of being on that flight. I really enjoyed her work. Did you see the movie she made with Jack Benny, the one that made fun of Hitler?"

Mauch's eyes darted around the restaurant.

"Relax, Ralph. No one here is going to shoot you for enjoying Hollywood poking fun at the Führer."

Mauch took a sip of his coffee. "So, the papers are gone?"

"Not at all. They were in a fireproof container. Covered in snow, no doubt. But we can go out there and look for them in the spring." He popped a chip into his mouth. "You sure you don't want a sandwich?"

"I've got to get back home." Mauch slid out of his seat.

Bauer caught the sleeve of his jacket. "Tell your boss I want certain pieces of art in payment this time." Reaching into his inside pocket, he retrieved the list and handed it over.

Mauch scanned the handwritten note, then looked back at Bauer with wide eyes. "These things come from the Amber Room."

Bauer smiled. "You just see that he gets that. And tell him when I come through, the price will seem like a bargain."

CHAPTER 24

Saturday, March 28, 1942

1:10 PM

Brownsville, Texas

Dressed in a brown suit, matching pumps, a large-brimmed hat, and sunglasses, Helen Meeker sat in a chair in the lobby of the Raleigh Hotel, pretending to read a movie magazine. Beside her, Henry Reese, the swelling and bruising now almost gone from his face, had his head buried in a newspaper.

"You reading about our deaths?" she asked with a grin.

"No. I already scanned that article. You got way too much ink, and I was only a footnote. So I moved on to the sports page. Joe Louis knocked out Abe Simon in the sixth round to retain the heavyweight crown last night in New York. I'm surprised it took that long. No one can touch the Brown Bomber."

As Reese continued to chatter about the world of sports, Meeker glanced back to the table where Henry Kranz was nibbling on his lunch. She studied the man for a moment. He appeared to be about fifty and athletic. He wore large, thick-rimmed glasses and had a dark, neatly trimmed beard. His shoulders were wide and his back straight. There was a mature charm about him.

"Henry, how tall would you say Kranz is?"

Reese glanced up. "Six foot or so. About my height."

"And your build too."

"He's a bit thicker in the middle." He winked.

Meeker leaned close. "I've got a plan."

Reese set the newspaper to one side. "I'm all ears."

"I'm going to gather the team in our room. You follow Kranz back to his. Even if you have to bind and gag him, you keep him there."

"What's this all about?"

"You just do your part. I'll take care of the rest."

CHAPTER 25

Saturday, March 28, 1942

7:35 PM

Brownsville, Texas

Helen Meeker smiled as Rebecca Bobbs put the last bit of makeup on Henry Reese. He slipped on Jacob Kranz's glasses and placed the man's hat on his head.

"Well, what do you think?" Bobbs asked as she stepped back from the frowning man sitting in the hotel room chair.

Meeker glanced from the agent's face to Jacob's. Though they'd never pass as identical twins, they looked similar enough. She hoped. "I think we have a good chance of pulling this off."

Bobbs sighed. "I haven't done any kind of theatrical makeup since college."

Meeker turned to her. "Fortunately, the instructions called for a meeting outdoors, at night. And they've never met Kranz face-to-face." She looked back at Henry. "How's your accent?"

"I can speak American as well as any other German," he assured her with a guttural twang to his voice.

Barnes, leaning against the far wall with his arms folded, shook his head. "Maybe you'd better not talk too much. Just act distressed a lot."

"Do you really think it will work?" the real Reggie Fister asked, wringing his hands.

Meeker put a hand on his shoulder. "Your brother has never seen Kranz in person, only in photos."

"Assuming they believe your agent is Jacob Kranz, what will they do to him?"

"Take him to the girl. If she confirms that he's her father, they'll likely try to put him on a plane bound for Mexico."

Kranz groaned. "And what if they find out the young man isn't me?"

"In their eyes, Henry is expendable. He's not an economic guru funding the underground, like you are. But don't worry. He's tough. He'll survive."

Kranz stiffened. "But if they uncover this charade, they will take my daughter to Germany and put her in a concentration camp."

Meeker moved to where the man sat on the queen-sized bed. "No, they won't. Your daughter is a pawn. If they think they've got you, they'll have no more need of her and let her go. If they realize they don't have you, they'll continue to use her as bait."

Kranz did not look relieved.

On the other side of the room, Reese studied Bobbs's handiwork in a mirror. "You know, I'm beginning to think this plan of yours just might work."

It had to. "When they take you, we'll do our best to follow you. But we'll have to stay pretty far back so they don't spot us. If we lose you, it'll be up to you to save the girl."

"Yeah, and since they'll probably search me, I won't be able to have a gun on me. Guess I'll have to survive on my wits."

"That's a scary thought." Meeker grinned, but as she leaned into his shoulder, she couldn't bear the thought of losing him again.

"Hey," Barnes said, "where's Fister?"

Helen glanced around the small hotel room. The man was nowhere in sight.

CHAPTER 26

Saturday, March 28, 1942

9:00 PM

Brownsville, Texas

Henry Reese walked out of the hotel into the moonlit night. He crossed the nearly empty street to a five-and-dime store that had been closed for three hours. Pulling Jacob Kranz's hat low over his forehead, he stopped on the sidewalk, outside the direct light of a streetlamp.

A few seconds later, a light-colored sedan parked a half block down the street switched on its lights and slowly rolled toward him. It stopped in front of the store, and a large man, dressed in dark pants and a plaid sports coat, stepped out of the front passenger seat. The top three buttons of his shirt were undone, revealing a hairy chest. His pointed boots looked to be at least a size thirteen.

The stranger quickly covered the three steps separating them, then studied Reese's face in the dim light. After glancing both directions to make sure they were alone, he frisked the agent and then pointed toward the car. As Reese approached, the back door opened. No one had to tell him to get in.

"Welcome, Mr. Kranz," a familiar voice called out from the other side of the backseat. "My name is Fister."

Even though he knew the man, Reese didn't respond.

"I'm glad you decided to do this the smart way." Fister looked to the driver. "Let's go, Hector. We have a plane to catch."

"My daughter?" Reese whispered.

"She's fine," Fister assured him. "You'll see her soon."

"And then you will let her go?"

Fister grinned. "My dear Mr. Kranz, you should know better than to make a deal with the devil. Your daughter will be accompanying you back to the land of your birth."

The Buick sedan headed south. Several miles down the road, Fister ordered the driver to make a U-turn.

CHAPTER 27

Saturday, March 28, 1942

11:00 PM

Outside of Brownsville, Texas

After traveling for a dozen miles or so, the sedan pulled up to a small adobe farmhouse. With two men in the front seat and Fister in the back, Reese had remained quiet during the trip. Now it was time to size up the operation and formulate some kind of plan.

After the driver shut off the eight-cylinder engine, Fister stepped out and looked at the large tin building a hundred yards to the south. "Hector, take our guest to the plane. I'm going to step inside, make a phone call, and get the girl."

As the big man yanked him from the seat, Reese took in the barren Texas landscape. It was going to be hard for any car to approach without being seen. So even if Meeker and the team had managed to tail them, it was doubtful they could make a surprise entrance. It appeared this plan was going to be up to him to pull off. And with two guns pointed at his back, the odds weren't good.

"You got a cigarette?" Reese asked Hector.

The big man didn't respond.

"How about you?" he asked the other man.

He remained mute too.

Reese didn't smoke. He just hoped a little small talk would loosen up his guards. No such luck.

Hector pointed his revolver toward a small metal building. When Reese didn't move, the man shoved the barrel into his back.

"I get the point," he snapped, then started walking.

The full moon revealed a dirt lane behind the shed. *Must be the runway.* With no wind or clouds, it would be easy to take off tonight.

As they approached the building, three more armed men stepped out. Reese saw no way out of this mess. Once the plane was in the air, he could try to overpower the pilot and take charge. But since he didn't know how to fly, there was a large downside to that idea.

A door opened and Hector pushed him inside the makeshift hangar, revealing a black DC-2. Only a few of these babies had been put into production before they were replaced. "Are you sure this is safe?"

None of the armed men responded.

The trio that met them at the shed opened the building's back door and pushed the plane outside. A lanky man dressed in flight gear stepped through a side door. "You must be Mr. Kranz."

Reese nodded.

"As soon as Fister gets here, we'll take off."

"Where are we going?" Reese asked.

"We have a rendezvous with a sub that will take you to Germany. I hear they're going to throw a big party for you when you arrive."

The guy didn't sound like a Nazi. Reese figured he must be a paid contractor, someone who worked for money, not causes. Life was safer that way. No matter who won, men like this would always have work. And stay alive.

The pilot looked at Hector. "Tie his hands. I don't want him causing problems on the flight."

The big man practically yanked Reese's shoulders from their sockets as he secured his wrists behind his back. He'd just finished tying the knots when Fister walked in.

"Where's the girl?" the pilot asked.

Fister smiled. "I'm keeping her here for a while. After I take advantage of her charms, I'll kill her."

Reese gulped, torn between voicing a complaint, as any distraught father would do, and causing Fister to examine him more closely. Best to remain quiet and appear resigned, at least for the moment.

"Your call," the pilot muttered. "Let's get the package on the plane and get out of here." He headed for the exit.

"Not so fast," Fister ordered. "I just got word the sub is late. We're supposed to delay takeoff for forty-five minutes."

"That wasn't the deal," the pilot snarled.

"Would you rather wait on the bench, where the Mexican officials might drive up and start asking questions?"

The man frowned at Fister. "At least put Kranz on the plane."

"Fine." Fister nodded at Hector. "Take him out there and tie him to his seat. I'm going to have a cup of coffee."

CHAPTER 28

Saturday, March 28, 1942

11:45 PM

Outside of Brownsville, Texas

"How many do you see?" Helen Meeker asked as she crouched on a small rise overlooking the adobe house, the metal barn, and acres of farmland.

Clay Barnes pulled the binoculars away from his face. "Six hired guns, a pilot, and Fister."

"Do you see Henry or the girl?"

"No. They might already be on the plane, or perhaps in the house."

"You stay here." She turned to Bobbs. "Rebecca, Dr. Ryan and I will circle around to the left and look in the house. If they're there, we'll bring them back."

"You sure you don't want me to come with you?" Barnes asked.

"Absolutely." She smiled. "You're the best shot, and we might need some cover."

He nodded.

"Okay, gang, let's go."

Within two minutes, the trio had made their way down the hill to the small home. The back door was unlocked. With her Colt ready, Meeker led the way through the kitchen and into the front room. Sitting on a small couch, curled up like a puppy, was Jacob Kranz's daughter.

Meeker signaled for the frightened young woman to remain quiet as Ryan and Bobbs checked the other three rooms.

"There's no one else here," Bobbs called out.

Meeker rushed to Suzy and gently touched her face. "Are you all right?"

"Yes," she whispered. "How's my dad?"

"He's safe."

A loud rumbling noise came from outside.

"They're firing up the engines on the plane," Bobbs announced.

"You two get Miss Kranz back to Barnes," Meeker ordered.

"It won't take both of us to do that," Bobbs argued. "I can go with you."

"No. Our job is to save the girl and her father. You make sure she's safe."

"Where are you going?" Barnes asked.

"To see if I can free Henry."

Not waiting for the argument she was sure would follow, Meeker hurried through the kitchen and back out the rear door.

Though the area between her and the plane was wide open with no cover and the moon was full and bright, she'd caught a break. There was no one outside the building.

She sprinted across the dirt to the shed. Pressing herself flat against the metal wall, she peered around the side.

"We're taking off *now*," a man shouted. "Plane's ready, motors are fired up, and it's been forty-five minutes. Let's get this over with."

"We wait until midnight." Fister's voice sent chills up Meeker's back. "I want to give the sub plenty of time to get to the rendezvous point."

"I'm not sitting around here any longer," the man roared. "My instructions were to take you and that Kranz guy, and I'm leaving now. You can either get on the plane or be left behind."

"Fine," Fister grumbled. "I'll grab my bag."

The pilot bolted out the back door and hurried to the DC-2. A few moments later, Fister emerged from the shed, suitcase in hand. After saying something to the men, he watched them shut the large doors. Then he made his way to the black plane. With a final look around, he entered the aircraft. Surprisingly, he didn't bother shutting the door.

Seizing the opportunity, Meeker raced toward the plane's open entrance with two objectives on her mind. The first was to free Henry Reese. The second was to make sure Alistair Fister did not escape.

The twin engines stirred up clouds of Texas dust as she approached the rear of the plane and crept toward the side door. With gun drawn, she took a deep breath and leaped inside. Two revolvers greeted her, both aimed at her forehead.

"Drop it, Helen," Fister ordered.

Before she had a chance to comply, the pilot kicked the Colt out of her hand. It skidded across the floor, coming to rest under one of the back rows.

Fister ordered Meeker to take the seat next to Kranz. After she complied, he turned to the pilot, who had retrieved her gun. "Get this plane off the ground."

As the man rushed to do as he'd been told, Fister turned back to Meeker and grinned. "You're going to love Berlin in the spring."

The President's Service Series

Made in the USA
San Bernardino, CA
26 March 2017